This book belongs to a **DIFFERENCE MAKER.**

Nalan

_____

Name

MALIK'S BIG DREAM
FUTURE AUTHORS CONTEST
WINNER

Aryanna Schrader
6th Grade
Three Rivers
Elementary School

CONGRATULATIONS!

MALIK
THE DIFFERENCE MAKER

STORY BY **LaMarqué D. Ward Sr., M.Ed.**
PICTURES BY **Aaron J. Ratzlaff**

DREAM BUILDERS UNIVERSITY PRESS

I would like to dedicate Malik The Difference Maker to YOU! To the student who has been bullied and learned how to forgive. You are a true champion! You have learned to let LOVE flow through you even when it is difficult. In your school and community you will need to continue to let your LOVE shine through. And remember, because of you, the world is a better place!

It was Monday morning at Thomasville Elementary school. Malik felt like things were going to be different today. In fact, Malik couldn't help but feel as if he was a different person. He walked through the hallways with his head held high and a smile on his face—he even greeted his teachers and classmates with a smile. Some of the students gave him odd looks while others just smiled politely or nodded in his direction.

"Good morning," Malik said, smiling at his history teacher, Mr. Wilson.

Mr. Wilson looked over at Malik before he smiled back at him. "Good morning, Malik. How are you this morning?"

"I'm doing great, Mr. Wilson," Malik said.

"Well, I'm happy to hear that. It's nice to see students in a good mood, even on a Monday morning." Mr. Wilson replied.

"Yeah, I'll see you in history," Malik replied before he walked over to his locker.

As he grabbed his books from his locker, he noticed Kevin walking down the hallway.

After their last encounter, Malik dreaded the thought of seeing Kevin again, but he refused to let thoughts of Kevin get the best of him. Not today.

Just don't let him get to you, Malik told himself.

"Well if it isn't Malick," Kevin said in a mocking tone.

"It's pronounced Malik," Malik corrected, glaring at Kevin.

"Whatever," Kevin rolled his eyes. "What difference does it make whether I call you Malick or 'new kid'?"

"It does make a difference. If you're gonna say my name, say it right."

"Hey," Kevin took a step forward and knocked Malik's books out of his hands. "You better watch yourself. I don't take kindly to being bossed around, especially by some new kid."

Malik could feel tightness in his chest as Kevin glared at him, but Malik stood his ground. "Telling you how to pronounce my name isn't being bossy."

Before Kevin could respond, the school bell rang, signaling that class was about to begin.

"You don't know how lucky you are," Kevin said before he walked off in a huff.

Malik couldn't help but sigh in relief as Kevin disappeared down the hallway. There was only so much taunting and bullying he could take from Kevin. Once he was sure Kevin was gone, he gathered his books from the floor and walked to his first class of the day.

After having four back-to-back classes, Malik was more than ready for lunch. Today, they were serving his favorite meal: pepperoni pizza with extra cheese. His eyes sparkled in delight as he spotted the pizza in the cafeteria. He grabbed a lunch tray and stood in line before grabbing a slice of pizza, milk, corn, and a chocolate pudding cup.

Where should I sit? Malik thought, scanning the tables in the cafeteria.

Before he could decide where to sit, Malik suddenly spotted Kevin sitting at the table in the back of the room. When their eyes met, Malik could feel a wave of dread wash over him as Kevin stood up and approached him.

"What do you want now, Kevin?" Malik asked.

"Just helping myself," Kevin replied, snatching Malik's pudding cup off his tray.

"I didn't say you could have that!"

"I wasn't asking." Kevin tore off the lid from the pudding cup before he licked it off.

"Just give me my pudding cup, Kevin. You can keep the lid."

"Oh, okay." Kevin smiled before he turned the pudding cup upside down and slapped it down on Malik's pepperoni pizza, covering it in chocolate pudding.

"Hey!"

"What, you said you wanted your pudding cup back. I just gave it back to you."

"That's not what I meant and you know it."

"Sorry, guess you should have been more specific. Thanks for sharing though."

As Malik watched Kevin walk away, he clenched his teeth and fists in frustration. It was at that moment that he decided if he was going to stand up to Kevin, he couldn't do it alone.

After lunch, Malik decided to visit the principal's office to ask for advice on his bullying problem. He was nervous, since it was his first time visiting the principal's office. As he stood in front of the door, Malik felt his throat drying and his palms getting sweaty. After taking a deep breath, he sighed before he knocked on the door.

"Come in," a female voice answered behind the door.

Malik opened the door before he stepped inside the office and closed the door behind him. When Malik turned around, he saw his principal, Maria Lopez, sitting behind her desk. A wave of relief washed over him as she greeted him with a smile.

"Hello, Principal Lopez," Malik said, returning the smile.

"Hello, Malik," Principal Lopez replied. "What brings you to my office today?"

"To tell you the truth, I actually have a bit of a problem."

"Well, why don't you tell me about your problem, and we'll find a solution to it."

Malik went quiet for a moment before he nodded his head and explained the trouble he had with his bully, Kevin. The principal remained silent until Malik finished speaking.

"Malik, exactly how long has this been going on?" Principal Lopez asked.

"This has been going on since I got here."

"Oh, really?" Principal Lopez looked at Malik with surprise before she shook her head sadly. "Well, this is just unacceptable. Whether it's physical or verbal, bullying is not something I tolerate at this school."

"I wish I hadn't tolerated the bullying for this long."

"Malik, there's no need to blame yourself. If anything, I'm responsible for not noticing this issue in my school sooner. The fact that you've come to me about your problem shows that you have the courage to stand up for yourself and ask for help."

"Thanks, Principal Lopez."

Malik couldn't help but feel as if a great weight had been lifted from his shoulders. He had finally found the courage to ask for help and take a stand against the bullying—but the feeling vanished, once Principal Lopez spoke again.

"I'll definitely need to get to the bottom of this. Would you be able to stop by my office after school today so we can discuss this further?" Principal Lopez asked.

"Sure, I can do that," Malik said with a short nod.

"Great, I'll make sure that Kevin will be here after school so I can discuss this with him as well."

In that moment, coming to the principal for help felt like a mistake. Kevin was the last person he wanted to talk to, much less see.

The school bell rang, signaling the end of the day. Students rushed to their lockers to grab their belongings and leave, but Malik was in no hurry. Now that the school day was over, he had to face what he was dreading since he left the principal's office: Kevin. After Malik told the principal about being bullied, Kevin was called to the principal's office an hour later.

I wonder just how mad he'll get when he sees me, since I told on him. Malik thought.

Malik's question was answered as he walked to the principal's office and saw Kevin standing outside her door.

"Well, if it isn't Malick, or should I say Mr. Snitch," Kevin said, shooting a glare at Malik. "Thanks to you, I got detention."

"How is it my fault that you got detention?"

"Because you were being a snitch!"

"If you hadn't been picking on me in the first place, this wouldn't have happened."

"You're making a big deal over nothing. All I did was call you names and–"

"Kevin, that's enough," A female voice interrupted the boys.

Malik and Kevin stopped and turned around to see Principal Lopez standing behind them, her arms folded across her chest in disapproval.

"Let's continue this discussion in my office," Principal Lopez said before opening the office door.

The boys exchanged glances before they walked into her office and both sat down in a chair.

"So, do you boys know why I brought you both in here after school today?" Principal Lopez asked.

"Well, sort of," Malik said with a shrug.

"Not really," Kevin said with a pout.

"Well then, let me explain further why you're both in here together. You both understand that verbal or physical bullying will not be tolerated in this school, correct?"

The boys both nodded, reluctantly.

"Since you two understand this, I want to make a proposal: a project that involves the two of you working together."

Malik looked at Kevin before he looked at Principal Lopez as if she had grown a second head.

Work on a project with Kevin? What's she talking about? Malik thought.

"What kind of project?" Kevin asked.

"Whatever you want the project to be on," Principal Lopez smiled. "As long as the topic you choose is something educational, school-appropriate, and you both agree on the topic."

Malik wasn't interested in working with Kevin on the project. After everything Kevin put him through, Malik didn't like the idea of working with him. It didn't surprise him when Kevin immediately expressed disinterest in the project.

"But why should I have to work on the project with him of all people?"

"You're right, Kevin. You don't have to work with Malik on this project, and I don't want to force you to do something you don't want to do. That's why I'm giving you a choice. You can either put aside whatever differences you have with Malik and work together on this project, or you can sit in detention for the next month. Considering you've been picking on Malik for about a month now, that sounds like a fair punishment, doesn't it?"

Kevin opened his mouth to speak to protest, but eventually decided not to say a word. For once, Kevin didn't have a comeback.

Wow, I didn't know Kevin had a whole month of detention. It almost makes me feel sort of sorry for him. Almost... Malik stole a glance at Kevin who was pouting in his chair.

"The both of you will have to come to an agreement to work on this project in order to make it happen," Principal Lopez said. "If one of you decides not to participate in this project, I'll dismiss the project and Kevin will keep his month of detention. I'm sure you both will need some time to think about this, so I'll give the two of you until tomorrow after school to make your decision."

"Okay, that sounds fair," Malik said.

"Good. You two come by my office tomorrow once you've reached a decision." Principal Lopez stood up from her desk to open the door and let Malik and Kevin out of her office.

"I guess if the principal doesn't need us for anything else, I'm going home. We can tell the principal tomorrow we're not going to do the project and that will be the end of it," Malik said before he began to walk down the empty hallway.

"Hey, wait!" Kevin quickly followed behind Malik. "You're not seriously going to let me sit in detention for a whole month, are you?"

"Why shouldn't I? You've been picking on me for a whole

month now, so I think that's only fair. Besides, I know you'd only agree to do this project with me to get out of detention then go right back to picking on me the minute it's over."

"But I—" Malik cut Kevin off before he could finish his sentence.

"I've made up my mind. Have fun in detention." Malik stuck his tongue out at Kevin before he walked down the hallway and out of the school.

"Home sweet home," Malik sighed, as he slipped his shoes and backpack off by the door.

After another day of being picked on and having back-to-back classes, Malik was ready to rest and relax. When he heard his mother call him into the kitchen, he realized he couldn't relax just yet.

"Sorry I'm home so late, Mom," Malik said as he walked into the kitchen. "I got called into the principal's office after school today."

Malik's mother looked at her son with surprise. Until today, Malik had never been to the principal's office. "Why did you get called to the principal's office?"

"The principal wanted to give me and this other student a project so that we could protest bullying by working together."

"Sounds like something that could be really great."

"Yeah, but I don't think I'm gonna do it."

"Why don't you want to do it?"

"I have to work on the project with another student that I don't exactly get along with."

Malik's mother looked at him with surprise. This was the first time Malik had complained to his mom about another student in school. In his mother's eyes, Malik was doing perfectly fine and insisted that school was "good."

"Why don't the two of you get along?" she questioned.

"Well, it's kind of a long story," Malik sighed.

"I've got time. Why don't we talk it over while we eat some ice cream?"

"Yes, please."

His mother laughed before she walked to the fridge to grab the chocolate chip ice cream, a bowl, and a spoon. Once she put the ice cream in a bowl and offered one to Malik, he went on to explain why he didn't get along with Kevin. After Malik finished telling his story, his mother reached out and ruffled his hair.

"Malik, that's just awful. I wish there was something I could have done to help you," she said.

"It's not your fault, Mom," Malik said, eating a scoop of ice cream. "Just listening to what I have to say is enough for me."

"But I'm proud of you for being brave enough to go to the principal about it. I know that wasn't easy for you," his mother smiled.

"It definitely wasn't. To be honest, I don't want to do the project with Kevin. I know he would only agree to do the project with me to get out of detention. Why should I do that after everything he's done?"

"I can understand why you wouldn't want to work on a project with someone who was picking on you. What did Kevin think about doing the project?"

"Kevin didn't say he was against the project, but I didn't bother to ask him about it because I just assumed he'd only want to do it to get out of detention."

"Did you ever consider maybe listening to his opinion about the project? Maybe he's got a few good ideas to contribute."

"I guess I never thought about that," Malik shook his head. "I never stopped to think he might actually have an idea for the project."

"Why not give him a chance and hear him out?

You might be surprised what happens when you give someone a second chance."

Malik stared into his bowl of ice cream, stirring it around with his spoon. The more he thought about it, the more Malik wanted to know what Kevin thought about the project or any ideas he had.

Maybe he's got some good ideas, but does he really deserve a second chance? Malik thought.

"Well, the principal gave you until tomorrow to make your decision. Why don't you think about it and talk it over with Kevin tomorrow?"

Malik spent the rest of the day mulling over his decision to work with Kevin on the project.

The next day, Malik's morning got off to a rocky start. After tossing and turning in bed the night before, thinking about the project and working with Kevin, Malik wasn't able to get much sleep.

I hope I can stay awake long enough to get through all my classes. I'm exhausted. Malik covered his mouth as he yawned.

After getting off the school bus, Malik walked inside the school and headed to his locker. When he got there, he found Kevin waiting.

"What are you doing here?" Malik looked at Kevin with a mixture of confusion and surprise.

"I want to talk to you about yesterday," Kevin mumbled under his breath.

"What did you say?" Malik could hardly hear Kevin mumbling with the other students talking amongst themselves.

"I want to talk to you about yesterday," Kevin shouted, causing a few students to look in his direction.

"Okay, okay, I get it," Malik put his hands over his ears. "Not so loud."

"Look, I'm not used to doing this sort of thing, so listen up," Kevin shoved his hands in his pockets, rocking back and forth on his feet. "I just wanted to say...that I get why you wouldn't want to work with me on this project. I haven't exactly been easy to put up with."

Malik couldn't believe his ears. He almost pinched his arm to make sure he wasn't dreaming.

"If you're willing to let bygones be bygones, I'm willing to do this project and give you any ideas I come up with, as long as you agree to do your fair share. I don't exactly like doing big school projects, but I'd rather do a group project than sit in detention by myself."

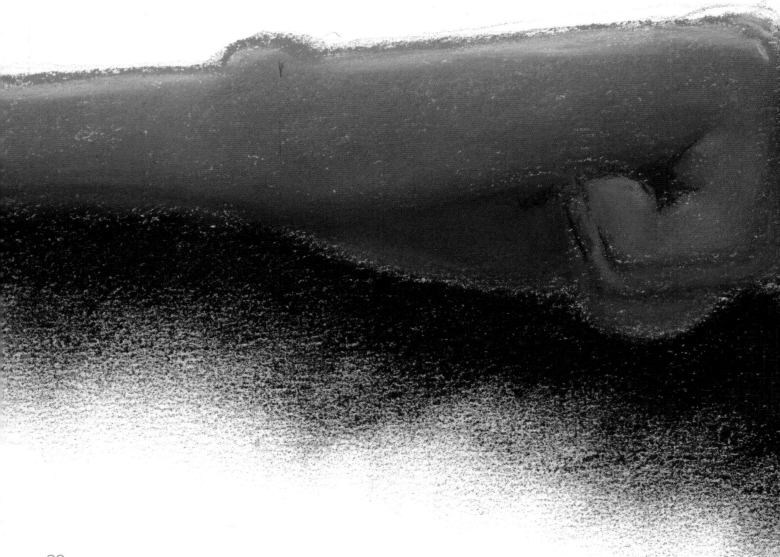

Malik stared at Kevin, completely stunned by his words. Malik couldn't find the words to speak.

"So, do we have a deal?" Kevin's words pulled Malik from his thoughts before he nodded his head.

"It's a deal," Malik made his hand into a fist before he held it out toward Kevin. "You've got yourself a partner."

Kevin looked down at Malik's fist before he laughed and bumped his own fist against it.

After classes ended, Malik and Kevin went to meet with Principal Lopez to discuss their decision to work on the project together and brainstorm ideas.

"I'm glad to see you two have decided to work together," Principal Lopez said with a smile. "Have you two come up with any ideas so far?"

"Actually, we have," Malik replied. "Kevin and I talked about it this morning and we decided to do an anti-bullying project. We want to do this idea because we both understand bullying firsthand, and we could use the project to create an anti-bullying system for the school."

"That's an excellent idea," Principal Lopez nodded with approval.

"I even drew some designs for the project," Kevin opened his backpack before handing over a sketchbook filled with drawings. "I didn't have much time since I drew these during lunch, but you'll get the idea once you see them."

"These look great, Kevin," Principal Lopez complimented.

"Can I see them?" Malik asked, turning to Kevin.

"Sure, take a look," Kevin agreed.

Malik took the sketchbook once Principal Lopez finished looking through the sketches. He looked at each sketch, admiring the shapes and colors of each one.

"This is a good one," Malik pointed to the sketch that said "Stop Bullying" in big bubble letters with a red stop sign hanging above it.

"Thanks," Kevin said, taking back his sketchbook. "It's not my best work though."

"How about this: 'Stop Bullying and Live Like a Champ'?" Malik suggested.

"I think the 'Live like a Champ' could work, but we have to develop that concept," Kevin rubbed his chin in thought.

"You're right, if this is going to be an anti-bullying system, we have to decide what 'live like a champ' means."

"And we'll need a bigger space to work in if we're gonna keep working on this project."

"I agree; you'll both need more space to work with," Principal Lopez declared. "Why don't you two take your ideas and sketches into the art room down the hall? Mr. Langdon should still be in there and I'm sure he'd be willing to let you use some of the art supplies in the classroom."

Malik and Kevin looked at Principal Lopez before agreeing to her suggestion. After gathering their belongings, the boys said goodbye to Principal Lopez and made their way into the art room.

"So, we've got poster boards, markers, pencils, colored pencils, paper, scissors, and glue. Looks like we've got everything we need," Malik looked at all the art supplies he and Kevin organized on the art table.

"I'm glad Mr. Langdon is letting us use all this stuff, but I don't think we need all this. Some paper and colored pencils would've been fine," Kevin shook his head.

"You never know. Some of this stuff might come in handy," Malik said with a grin.

"I guess so," Kevin said, as he picked up a red colored pencil. "Why don't you tell me your ideas and I'll draw more sketches and we'll go from there?"

"Good idea." Malik grabbed a sheet of paper and started jotting down his ideas.

Malik and Kevin proceeded to work on their parts of the project silently. It wasn't until Malik's stomach grumbled that the silence was broken.

I wish I had brought a snack with me, Malik sighed under his breath.

Before Malik could complain how hungry he was, a chocolate pudding cup and a spoon was suddenly placed in front of him. Malik looked over at Kevin, taken aback by Kevin's generosity.

"What's this for?" Malik looked at Kevin.

"Well, you're hungry, aren't you?" Kevin said, raising an eyebrow. "You can't do this project on an empty stomach. Plus, I... guess I kind of owe you, after what I did to the last pudding cup you had."

"Oh…" Malik had almost forgotten about that incident in the cafeteria. "Well, thanks."

"Don't mention it," Kevin's lips curved into a small smile. "I'm curious though…"

"About what?"

"What made you change your mind to work on this project with me? After everything I put you through?"

Malik went quiet for a moment, thinking back to the conversation he had with his mom the day before.

"A wise woman once told me you'd be surprised by what happens when you forgive and give someone a second chance." Malik said.

"So, you're saying you've forgiven me for all that stuff I did to you?"

"Yes, you're forgiven, Kevin. You've shown me, despite everything you've said or done to me, that when you give someone a second chance and forgive them, sometimes they're willing to change a little."

"Well… thanks," Kevin said as he sheepishly rubbed the back of his neck. "Thanks for giving me a second chance."

"And thank you for the pudding cup," Malik chuckled, eating a spoonful of pudding.

"You don't have to make such a big deal out of it. It's just pudding," Kevin said and shook his head in amusement.

After Malik finished his pudding, he and Kevin resumed brainstorming and sketching out ideas for the *Live like a Champ* anti-bullying campaign before combining their ideas.

"I think this is a pretty cool looking campaign design, if I do say so myself." Kevin looked down at the three individual posters they created.

"Yeah, the pictures you drew really go with the words," Malik complimented before reading over the words on the posters. "Think before you act, you think like a champ. Speak out against bullying to speak like a champ. And act like a champ by taking action against bullying. Follow these rules and you'll live like a champ."

"I don't know about you, but I think we should think like champs and call it a day for now. We've done more than enough brainstorming for one day."

"I agree. Let's show the principal what we've created later."

"It's a deal, partner." Kevin made his hand into a fist and held it up to Malik.

Malik brought his fist up and gently bumped it against Kevin's fist.

One week later, Malik and Kevin presented their final poster designs to Principal Lopez before she gave them permission to make copies and hang them up in the hallways.

"The project has come together pretty nicely," Malik said as he taped a poster to the wall.

Not only had the project come along, but Malik and Kevin were also gradually getting along better than they were before.

"I think so too," Kevin replied, hanging up another poster. "But do you think we'll really make a difference, once the project is finished?"

Malik turned to Kevin and grinned. "I bet once we've finished this project, we'll make such a difference that the whole school will call us the Difference Makers."

"Oh, really?" Kevin laughed, shaking his head. "So, we're superheroes of Thomasville Elementary now?"

"Not without capes we aren't," Malik grinned.

"Fine, fine," Kevin said jokingly. "I'll sketch our cape designs and we'll hire a tailor to make them for us, okay?"

"That's the best idea I've heard all day."

"Hey, Kevin!" an unfamiliar voice suddenly shouted.

When Kevin looked toward the direction of the voice, he spotted one of his classmates, Conner, walking towards him.

"What do you want, Conner?" Kevin asked. "I'm in the middle of something."

"I bet it's not more important than what I'm about to do with these," Conner said, holding up a pair of beige ballet shoes.

Malik looked at the ballet shoes in Conner's hands. "So... you're going to dance?"

"What?" Conner looked at Malik confused before he frowned and glared at Malik. "No! Are you, stupid? I've got something planned for these shoes. Not that it's any of your business."

"Hey, watch what you say about my friend!" Kevin shot a glare right back at Conner.

Malik and Conner both looked at Kevin with complete surprise.

He thinks of me as a friend...? Malik believed Kevin considered him to be a partner for a school project, but never would've imagined Kevin would consider him a friend.

"What, this dork is your friend?" Conner laughed. "Since when?"

"That's none of your business," Kevin retorted. "What are you doing with those shoes anyway?"

"Remember that kid in our math class that takes ballet classes after school?"

"You mean Evan?"

"Yeah, that kid. He left his shoes in the locker room in gym today, so I thought I'd hang them on a power line."

"What would be the point in doing that?"

"Wouldn't it be hilarious to see that twinkle toes try to jump and reach to get his shoes back? So why don't you do me favor and ditch that loser friend of yours and help me hang these?"

Malik looked between Kevin and Conner, unsure of what to do. Before Malik could say something, Kevin approached Conner and snatched the ballet shoes out of his hands.

"You're right, let's ditch this guy and finish hanging up these posters, Malik." Kevin said.

"What did you just say?" Conner looked completely insulted by Kevin's words.

"You heard me," Kevin said. "I'm gonna finish hanging up these posters with Malik then we're gonna give the shoes that you stole back to Evan."

"You can't be serious," Conner said.

"Would telling Principal Lopez what you were about to do be serious enough for you?" Malik threatened.

"Man, you two sure know how to ruin a guy's fun. Fine, I know when I'm outnumbered. I'm out of here." Conner huffed angrily before stomping off.

When Malik could no longer see Conner, Malik turned to Kevin and smiled.

"Way to live like a champ back there, Kevin," Malik congratulated.

"Thanks. Right back at you," Kevin returned the smile. "I think this 'Live like a Champ' campaign could catch on."

"Kevin, after what you just did, I think it already has."

DREAM BUILDERS UNIVERSITY
STUDENT AFFIRMATION

I AM THE PROMISE OF TOMORROW

I AM THE HOPE OF TODAY

I BELIEVE IN MYSELF IN EVERY WAY

I WON'T GIVE UP

I WON'T GIVE IN

I BELIEVE IN YOU

WITH YOU WE WIN

OUR WORLD IS A BETTER PLACE
WHEN WE START WITHIN

DREAM,

work hard,

work harder,

and work the hardest

until you see your DREAM.

Then work even harder.

- LaMarqué D. Ward Sr., M. Ed.

www.DreamBuildersUniversity.com